SANDRA'S ROSE

OTHER TITLES BY TARA C. GODDARD

SANDRA'S ROSE

TARA C. GODDARD

3

© *Goddard Collection 2020*

This is a work of fiction. Any resemblance to actual persons, or events is purely coincidental.

CHAPTER 1

The rugged army green truck made a sharp turn and suddenly the old man with the full beard and the stench of midday alcohol on his breath stopped. He put the gear in park and pointed down the street. Jacob had his earpiece in and didn't hear what the man said. In fact, he was not sure the man said anything. He turned his head and looked down the street where the gentleman was pointing to. The old man coughed and rubbed his hairy chin and then smiled.

"Boy, you're not too good at hearing, are you?" the man said. Jacob removed his earpiece.

"I'm sorry, I didn't hear what you said," Jacob said. He looked at his phone, it was half past one. "According to my GPS the Inn should be around here," Jacob added. The old man laughed. He grabbed the bottle of whiskey between his legs and took a swig.

"That's what I've been trying to tell you boy...the Inn is down the road. I gotta go in the other direction, so you're on your own from here out."

"Oh, I'm sorry...hey thanks man," Jacob said as he reached behind him and grabbed his duffle bag and backpack. "Are you sure I can't give you anything for the ride? Twenty bucks?"

"No, thank you, young man. Keep your money. A young boy like you needs to have money in his pockets. Makes life a little easier," the old man said and laughed, "Just walk right down there. The Inn is right past the lavender field," the old man said.

"Thanks, again," Jacob said. The old man winked at him as a group of young women in short skirts walked by him talking aloud. Jacob looked behind him to see what the old man was trying to communicate to him. "You pervert," Jacob said with a smile on his face.

"We're all perverts son. Even the women," he said and then abruptly put the gear back in drive and drove into the middle of the street, making a turn and driving in the opposite direction.

Jacob marveled at the old man's carefree attitude towards traffic. He was wary of getting in the truck at the train station when the old man asked where he was headed. He knew accepting the ride was in effect risking his own life. However, Jacob was in for the adventure. He wanted to have adventure for the summer, even though coming to Greenport was to work. He knew there was adventure to be had for a young man his age. The group of girls he saw walking by earlier were a signal to him that Greenport was not going to disappoint.

"Get out the way!" a young man on a bicycle shouted as he nearly drove into Jacob who was standing in the middle of the road appreciating the architecture of an old building that looked like it might have housed a bank in the past.

"Sorry," Jacob said and moved out of the way.

"Tourists," the rider said and rode on.

Jacob continued walking down the street, taking in the sights of the small town whose streets were bursting to the seams with people. His business class professor praised the town for its ability to provide a solid place to think during the winter while being full of life and energy during the summertime.

"Oh, that's beautiful," Jacob said as he stood in front of the lavender field. He took out his phone and snapped pictures of the field.

When Jacob reached the front of the Lavender Inn, he stood outside for a few minutes, taking pictures of the place. An old man with white sneakers on, sat outside by a small table, drinking coffee. He watched attentively as the young man took pictures of the exterior of the place. The inn had one main house where the office was located, but the rooms were behind the house, each with a view of the water behind them.

The old man laughed as Jacob tripped on his own bags and stumbled, stopping short of hitting his face on the concrete. He looked at the man and shook his head. The man shrugged. He then pointed to the front door of the house where an older Italian woman stood, holding the door.

"Young people these days," the old man said.

"Mr. Hagen leave the boy alone," the woman said.

"Mrs. Conti, I haven't done a thing. He fell on his own," the man said and took a sip of his coffee.

"You shouldn't drink coffee in the afternoon," Jacob said.

"Jacob Alexander?" Mrs. Conti said.

"Yes," he replied.

"Okay, great, you're a little late. I have to get going so get in here, your mother's been calling," Mrs. Conti said.

"Mama's boy," Mr. Hagen said and chuckled.

Jacob followed Mrs. Conti into the house. The place smelled fresh, like cleaning supplies. It was evident someone just cleaned it. Mrs. Conti removed her white blouse and Jacob turned and faced in the opposite direction so as to give her privacy. When she cleared her throat, he turned back around. She now had on a yellow short-sleeve shirt.

"Here's your key," she said and handed it to him. "You're going to be in room 5D. It's small, but I don't think you need much space. Every place around here is walkable so don't waste your money on trying to get a cab. My only rules are, don't break anything, keep the noise level down. And don't call me after 7 pm," she added and grabbed her handbag.

"Okay, thanks,"

"Breakfast is free. It's usually out between 7 am and 9. And call your mother," she said and left.

Bemused, Jacob grabbed his belongings along with the key Mrs. Conti gave him and headed for his room. It was a small room with a kitchenette, a bed in the middle, a medium sized flat screen television against the wall, and a small bathroom. It was the perfect sized room for him. He wasn't planning on being in the room for long during his stay in Greenport, so it did not matter what it looked like. He opened the backdoor that led to the little beach on the other side and stood in the doorway, listening to the crashing of waves.

"Jacob?" Maureen Alexander said when she answered the phone.

"Hey mom," he responded, "I'm here," he added.

"Oh, thank god, I was getting a little worried," she said.

"I'm fine mom. Everything is fine."

"Your sister wants to say hi," Maureen said. Then he could not hear her clearly. He heard arguing in the background.

"Hello?" he said. He wanted to go out in the town. Being on the phone was an unwelcome delay.

"Hey Jacob," he heard his sister say.

"Mom is such a liar. You didn't want to say hi to me," he said.

"Jacob...whatever, you're alright?" Julia said.

"I'm fine. I'm 19 now. I don't need anyone to hold my hand. I'm going to go out walking in the town. Tell mom I'll call her tomorrow," he said.

"Alright big man. Please don't...don't drink too much," Julia said. Jacob sighed.

"Bye sis, I'll catch you later," he said and hung up.

The town of Greenport was crawling with people when Jacob set out to walk to the little town center. The place was a typical east coast town with little houses right next to old churches with worn exteriors that no one thought to paint. He put his headphones in his ears and let the music provide a soundtrack for the self-guided tour he was embarking on. Cars zoomed past him as if there were no laws governing the place. Behind those wheels were young people like him. Though they had few responsibilities. He was there to work on a farm and to take advantage of a summer away from his mother and the problems that an over-caring parent can bring into a relationship.

At the edge of the town, just before the land spilled into the water, was a large carousel. Jacob recalled how much he loved carousels when he was a kid. He stood on the outside watching as children were led to the carousel by parents juggling a bag in one hand and a quickly melting ice cream cone in another. Jacob chuckled, amused by the length to which parents were willing to go to make their children happy.

He thought about going on the carousel, but worried that people would think he was weird for wanting to ride on a carousel, surrounded by children, given the fact that he did not have a child of his own.

"You know it's a little creepy just watching people with their children like this," a young woman who was now standing next to him said. Jacob removed his headphones and turned to look at her. She had long jet-black hair and brown eyes. She smiled at him.

"What are you part of neighborhood watch or something?' he asked. She chuckled. Then her face became stern and fixed.

"Yes, I am...and we got a report about a creepy blonde guy watching little kids get on a carousel," she said. Jacob looked around, just to make sure he wasn't suddenly surrounded by neighborhood watch people.

"I'm not doing anything wrong," he said.

"You sound defensive," she said.

"Dude, you just came and accused me of being creepy because I'm standing here minding my own business," he said and turned away from her.

"Did you just call me a dude?" the young woman said as she walked after him, her satchel swinging next to her body. Jacob stopped and turned to face her.

"What do you want? Are you begging for money?" he asked. She laughed. He thought she had a cute laugh, like a nervous person.

"I'm totally playing with you," she said, "you must be new around here," she added with a smirk.

"Are you infamous for accusing strangers of crimes around here?" he asked.

"No," she said.

"Then what is it?" he asked. She smirked.

"Nothing, buddy. I was bored," she said.

He turned and started walking away from her again. She scoffed as he walked off. He walked around the carousel to an area where bystanders stood, watching boats as they pulled in and out of the marina picking up passengers.

Though he found the sight of the water and the boats wading in it to be peaceful, Jacob thought about the weird dark-haired girl who was picking on him earlier. He hadn't immediately thought about it, but he came to realize that she was a beautiful girl and must have had a reason for wanting to talk to him. She had a weird approach, he thought, but it worked. Now he was interested in finding out more about her.

Jacob turned back and went to the area where he had been standing earlier. But she was not there. Then he looked over at the carousel. He watched as she rode on a carousel, her arms in the air bumping up and down on a statuesque horse with her arms in the air. He smiled. She waved at him.

He waited there, knowing that this might be his only chance to regain her attention. He did not know what to expect. Their earlier interaction suggested that she was not a normal girl. He feared he may have insulted her with his reaction to the things she said.

"Back to being a creep already?" she asked as she walked over to him. He chuckled.

"Have dinner with me tonight," he said. She laughed.

"Is that a joke? I don't even know you," she said.

"True, but we can change that." he said.

"I have to go meet my friend now," she said.

"I'm new here. I don't know anyone," he said.

"Bye blondie," she said and tapped him on the chest.

"What's your name?"

"Rose," she said as she started walking away from him.

"Am I going to see you around here again?"

"We'll have to leave that to fate buddy," she said and left.

Jacob lamented that he might have missed an opportunity with Rose by being so cold to her earlier. He put his headphones back on and continued walking through the town center. He walked in and out of the one grocery store, walking the aisles aimlessly, unaware of what the people in the place might have thought of a young man wandering. He walked by the fountains and ran his fingers through the water like he had done in Rome on vacation when he was a child.

He stopped his wandering when he saw the Limerick bar. He checked his pockets for the fake id that his sister procured for him. When he opened the door, he expected a bouncer of some sort to be waiting there to check his id. However, there was no one at the door. The place was packed with people. It was a mix of young people starting their summer vacations, dads aiming to escape the demands of family life for a brief moment, and locals for whom drinking hour was any hour of the day.

Jacob sat at the bar, trying his best to look inconspicuous. No one paid him attention. He might as well have been invisible. Then he caught the eye of the young bartender sliding drinks to other patrons who looked past their limits. She smiled at him. He tried his best to think nothing of it. She was working after all. She would not flash a frown at a paying patron.

"ID," she said before he could open his mouth to say a word. He coughed. He thought he'd been caught out before he was able to get a taste of alcohol in the bar. He reached inside his pockets and handed her the id. She looked at it and looked at him and then looked at it again.

"I shave sometimes," he said. She chuckled.

"You must think I'm an idiot kid," she said.

"You talk as if you're much older than me," he said.

"You're 25?" she asked.

"I'll have the best summer ale you have on tap," he said. She paused and looked around, as though she was in the middle of doing something wrong and didn't want to get caught. She slid the id back to him.

"Summer ale it is then," she said as she poured the drink, "new in town huh?"

"How do you figure?" he asked. She handed him the beer.

"Smooth, well moisturized hands, pretty face that hasn't seen the sun in months," she said.

"Oh, you think I'm pretty," he said and slid his blonde hair back.

"Oh, don't make the mistake of thinking I like you," she said, "that'll be seven dollars," she added. He chuckled.

"I don't get the pretty boy discount?" he asked.

"Hey Brea! Can I get another pitcher?" a bearded dark-haired gentleman at the other end of the bar shouted.

"So, your name is Brea," Jacob said and slid her a ten-dollar bill," keep the change" he added. She laughed.

"Oh, you're so generous sir," she joked as she grabbed the money. He was going to say something else, but she moved to the other end of the bar before his thoughts were formalized.

For the rest of the night Jacob tried his best to get Brea's attention, but the young woman paid little attention to him. She'd only respond to him when he was ordering another beer. And so Jacob kept ordering beers, in a vain attempt to get her to talk to him. And when he came close to emptying his pockets, Jacob gave up on his pursuit of the young brunette with the sharp tongue. He paid his last bill and walked out of the bar looking like a defeated man.

The night air was chilly but comfortable. He walked down the middle of the road towards the inn with reckless abandon, fortunate that there were very few cars on the road. He thought about how wonderful it would be to live in a town like Greenport where half the year few people are present and the other half it borders on overcrowded. He heard yelping sounds of youths celebrating the freedom one acquires away from the controlling eyes of parents.

An hour later, Jacob made his way back to the inn. He had gotten lost. The alcohol flowing through his veins made it hard to make the right decisions about which streets to turn on so he walked straight for a long time. Yet he managed to make his way back to the inn. As he was opening the door to his room, he heard footsteps. He quickly turned around and stumbled a little.

"So, this is where you're staying," Brea said. Jacob closed his eyes and opened them again.

"Hmm, so you're not from here are you?" he said as she got closer.

"And you're not twenty-five," she said.

"Minor...detail," he said. She chuckled.

"You're a funny guy,"

"No... what you said was that I was pretty," he said. She laughed. He walked closer to her.

"What are you doing?" she asked.

"I think you're pretty too," he said.

"Does that usually work for you?" she asked. He got a little closer.

"You think I'm doing this because I'm drunk...which I am drunk...definitely...but I think you are very pretty and tough and..." he stopped mid-thought and kissed her. She pushed him back.

"Good night Jacob," she said and smiled.

"I like you a lot," he said.

"We'll see," she said, "you'll get over that" she added and walked away.

The next morning, Jacob woke up with a pounding headache. His back hurt from the hard mattress he slept on. The sun pushed through the little space between the blinds. He sat up slowly, his eyes barely open. He nearly fell to the ground as he stepped off the bed. *I'm never drinking again.* He knew those words were false, but in the moment, with the way his body felt, it seemed like a good thought.

He thought about jumping into the shower, then he got a glance of the clock on the wall. It was 10 am. He was beyond late. He quickly brushed his teeth and changed his shirt and ran out of the door. Mrs. Conti shook her head when she saw him running. As he reached the curbside, Mr. Hagen suddenly showed up out of nowhere. Smoke came out of the pipe in the old man's mouth.

"What are you 100 years old?" Jacob said as he tried to move around Mr. Hagen.

"You're late," the older gentleman said as he rubbed his chin.

"Do you mind?" Jacob asked. Mr. Hagen laughed and stepped to the side.

Jacob managed to catch a cab to the Halimut Farm which was ten miles away from the town center. As he approached the property, he saw a middle-aged man in jeans and a blue t-shirt talking to a man on a tractor. Jacob stopped by the tractor and waited for both men to stop talking.

"Who are you?" the man in the blue shirt said.

"Jacob Alexander," Jacob said. The man nodded to the driver of the tractor signaling the end of their conversation. "When I employ someone, Jacob, I expect them to show up to work on time," he said.

"I'm sorry, I overslept, won't happen again," Jacob said.

"You reek of alcohol," the man said. Jacob hadn't noticed the scent of alcohol seeping through his pores. He was embarrassed that his new employer had to point that out. He did not respond to the comment, though he felt a natural need to apologize once more.

Mr. Halimut started walking towards a house on the property and Jacob followed behind him like a dog needing direction from its owner. The man occasionally glanced back to make sure the boy was keeping up with him. Jacob wondered what he would be asked to do. He had no real interest in farming, but he jumped at the chance to come to the farm as a way to spend his summer away from his family and to experience an environment he was not familiar with.

"Dr. Ridern spoke highly of you," Mr. Halimut said.

"Yeah, he's a great guy," Jacob said.

"I'm not quite sure what he sees in you," Mr. Halimut said. Jacob smiled. *Touché.*

"Dr. Ridern is my advisor," Jacob said, "he likes to look at the bright side of things," he added. Mr. Halimut scoffed.

"We all have our faults," Mr. Halimut said. Jacob knew then that working for this man wasn't going to be as easy as he had imagined.

When they reached the house, Mr. Halimut walked around the corner and came back with three cans of paint and a tarp. He looked at Jacob up and down and sucked his teeth and then went back around the corner again. He returned with a big apron covered in stains that looked like it had seen better days.

"Don't wear your nice clothes when you come here unless they mean nothing to you," Mr. Halimut said and handed him the apron.

"Thanks," Jacob said.

"You see that barn over there?" Mr. Halimut said as he pointed at a big barn with fading red paint.

"Yes sir?"

"Start painting it. Don't worry about the top, I don't want you climbing any big ladders. Just start working on the lower half. My other guys will take care of the top in the next few days," Mr. Halimut said. The older gentleman walked into the house before Jacob could utter another word.

"Friendly guy," Jacob said as he gathered the paint, the tarp and the apron as well as his bag and headed for the barn.

When he reached the barn, he noticed paint brushes on the floor. He picked up the paint brushes and wiped them up. Then he took a walk around the barn to get an idea of the task ahead. *I don't know the first thing about painting.* Jacob let out a loud laugh, and then looked around to make sure no one was around to see him laughing by himself. On the exterior of the barn, was a faucet with a bucket underneath. He figured he'd have to use some water during the process, so he grabbed the bucket and filled it.

"You don't know the first thing about painting, do you?" a woman said. Jacob looked up.

"Holy shit!" he exclaimed.

"Well I don't think I've had that response to my criticism before," the woman said. *Wow she is gorgeous.*

"You are absolutely beautiful," Jacob said. The woman had on a stern face as though his comment didn't travel through her ears.

"My husband likes to pick on the young kids that come work for him," the woman said.

"Oh, it's no big deal. I think he's a really nice guy," Jacob said. The woman laughed.

"That's adorable," she said. "You have a sense of humor. That's good." she added. Jacob put the bucket of water down.

"What's your name?" he asked.

"Mrs. Halimut," she said. He chuckled.

"No, your real name," he said. She smiled.

"Please make sure you don't show up hungover again. Or your summer will be very brief if you know what I mean," she said.

"You're not answering my question...I doubt you want to just be called Mrs. Halimut. That lacks identity," he said. She laughed.

"Are you one of those pop psychology students?" she asked.

"No, I'm just a guy who sees a beautiful woman hiding behind her husband," he said.

"You're brave kid,"

"Not at all. Just young and careless," he replied. She pulled her shawl down, covering her shoulders.

"Sandra," she said.

"I'm Jacob Alexander, pleased to meet you Sandra Halimut," he said and shook her hand.

"Goodbye Jacob, stay out of trouble," she said as she walked past him.

Jacob turned and watched her walk to the house. She turned around to see if the young man was still standing there and caught him staring at her. He did not blink. This amused her and she winked at him and entered the house.

Jacob stood there for a few minutes, mesmerized by the woman whose husband was the reason he was in town to begin with. Then he turned around to face the monumental task of having to paint the barn. Jacob plopped the cans of paint onto the tarp. Painting was the last thing on his mind. Yet he began his work in earnest, moving his paintbrush up and down as he lay the paint on the wooden barn.

He was on his first pass toward the barn door when he caught a glimpse of the jet-black hair, swinging as the young woman ran by the barn. Jacob stopped in his stride to watch as the young woman, with her phone to her ear, ran across to the house. *That's that girl I saw at the carousel yesterday.*

"Hey!" he shouted. The girl stopped and turned around. Then she smiled. It was her. He had been right.

"Hey weirdo," she said as she hung up the phone and started walking back towards him.

"Jacob's the name," Jacob said. "What are you doing here?" he added.

"I can ask you the same troublemaker," she said.

"Troublemaker? You have no idea what I'm capable of," he said. She scoffed.

"I can't believe my dad hired a goof like you," she said as she flicked her hair behind her.

"Your...dad? You're Halimut's daughter?" he asked, incredulous. She nodded.

"When I meet new people, I don't usually lead with being Brendan Halimut's daughter," she said. "You're doing a shit job by the way. My dad's not going to be happy about that," she added. Jacob laughed.

"Have dinner with me tonight," he said. She chuckled.

"Again with that? Dude you're like broke," she said.

"I'm not broke. You have to eat, don't you?" he asked. She laughed.

"You're cute, but...my dad...I'm sorry," she said, "I'm not allowed to date the working guys," she said with a sheepish smile on her face. Jacob smiled at her. He understood.

Jacob took a step back away from her and turned back to the barn. She stood there for a few minutes. He did not know why she stayed. He expected her to have gone inside the house, or elsewhere. Jacob was deliberate in not turning around to see her standing there, watching him. And after a few minutes, Rose walked away. It was then that he turned and watched her. *She looks so much like her mother, it's crazy.*

A few hours later, Jacob was laying on the grass in front of a row of tomatoes when he heard footsteps. He did not want to open his eyes. He had been painting for hours and this was the tiny little break he was afforded. He took a whiff of the air, wondering if it was Rose coming to bother him. When he opened his eyes, he saw a tall Latino man with a small beard standing over him. Jacob sat up quickly and began coughing. The man stared at him intently.

"Want some pineapple?" the man said as he handed Jacob a plastic container with chopped pineapples in it.

"Yeah, thanks man," Jacob said and grabbed a handful of chopped pineapple. The man sat on the grass across from Jacob.

"I'm allergic to grass," the man said. Jacob laughed.

"Is that true?"

"Yeah, funny huh?" the man said, "I'm Luis by the way," he added.

"Jacob,"

"I've heard," Luis said. Jacob laughed.

"I'm popular here already?" Jacob asked.

Both men watched as Sandra walked across the field to go to the strawberry fields. Both of their jaws dropped as they watched the woman standing by the strawberries, taking pictures. Luis tapped Jacob on the shoulder, but Jacob did not respond.

"Hey man you have to be careful," Luis said.

"Yeah, I'm sure she's not interested in me," Jacob said. Luis laughed.

"I'm talking about Rose. I saw you talking to her earlier," Luis said.

"Oh she's...she's,"

"She's flirting with you. And I'm telling you to stay clear of her or you'll end up losing your job. Her dad has a serious issue with anyone talking to her. Don't even say hi in front of him," Luis said. Jacob scoffed.

CHAPTER 2

Later that afternoon, Jacob labored to get back to the inn. He was tired. He had not worked that hard in all of his life. He thought about life on the farm as being nothing but hard toiling. He couldn't get what Mr. Halimut got from living this way. *Surely there are easier ways to make money.*

Mr. Hagen was sitting outside at a small table when Jacob arrived with his small backpack over his right shoulder. The smell of freshly brewed coffee filled his lungs as he watched the older man in a three-piece grey suit sip his afternoon coffee. Mr. Hagen, upon seeing Jacob, motioned for the young man to join him at the table. Jacob waved him away, concerned that the older gentleman wanted to pick on him. Mr. Hagen insisted.

"Please young Jacob, sit with me. Have some coffee," Mr. Hagen said as he got up half-way and pulled the chair for Jacob.

"I'm sorry. I can't drink coffee this late. Then I'd be up all night, I don't know how you do it," Jacob said. Mr. Hagen poured a little bit of coffee in a small cup and slowly slid it to Jacob.

"It's decaf. But the taste is excellent. Madame Conti made it," Mr. Hagen said. Jacob picked up the cup and inhaled the aroma of the arabica beans. "Here have some cannoli," Mr. Hagen added.

"You know, I could have sworn that you didn't like me," Jacob said. Mr. Hagen scoffed.

"That's an inconsequential thing to worry about," Mr. Hagen said as he bit into a piece of cannoli.

"Well..."

"Jacob, you're young. You're going to experience many things in your life. The older you get, the easier it becomes to understand that it doesn't matter if someone likes you or not," Mr. Hagen said and chuckled.

In the corner of his eye, Jacob saw Brea in a short maroon bikini and a cream-colored straw hat atop her head. She was talking to a young blond woman by a window. Mrs. Conti stepped outside and called the blonde woman to come inside. It was then that Brea finally saw Jacob at the table with Mr. Hagen. She waved at him. Mr. Hagen motioned for her to come join them.

"Brea come have some cannoli. Madame Conti made them just now," Mr. Hagen said. Jacob motioned for her to come.

"Well gentlemen, I don't want to interrupt whatever it is you have going on here," she said, "how are you today Jacob?" she added as they made eye contact. He smiled.

"Exhausted," he said. She laughed.

"Yeah I don't know why you thought it was a good idea to come work on a farm," she said.

"Hey there, is nothing wrong with hard work. It builds character," Mr. Hagen said. Brea chuckled.

"I'm going to head to the beach to watch the sunset and drink, come with?" she said. Jacob sighed. Mr. Hagen kicked him under the table.

"I didn't get an invite," Mr. Hagen said. Brea laughed. She bent over and kissed the older gentleman on the cheek.

"I love you Mr. Hagen, but stop staring at my boobs," she said. They all laughed.

"I'll meet you there in like 15 minutes? I have to grab something to eat really quick before Mrs. Conti yells at me," Jacob said.

"Cool," she said and rejoined the blonde girl in front of the inn.

A little later, after he had his fill of Mrs. Conti's risotto, Jacob returned to his room and put his things away. He took a quick shower and then headed to the beach via the back door in his room. The sun was setting, with a beautiful orange-red color on the horizon. It made it a little difficult to know exactly where Brea was. The beach was full of young and old people sitting on lawn chairs, watching the sun and listening to the waves as they swayed to their tranquil best.

He heard his name, and so he walked in the direction of the noise. Brea was sitting on a large beach towel with a pink panther design on it. She waved at him with a bottle of tequila in her hand.

"Come, come, have a sit. My friend just ditched me for some guy," she said and laughed, "I'm sorry, I started without you," she said as she handed him the bottle of tequila.

"That's alright, I'll catch up in no time," he said. She chuckled.

"It's beautiful out here," she said.

"You're beautiful," he said and took a swig of the tequila. She chuckled.

"Will you get off that already," she said looking at him, "you're younger than me," she added.

"Not by much. And also, that doesn't stop me from appreciating your beauty," he said. She laughed.

"There are lots of beautiful people here," she said.

"Yes, I've noticed,"

He took a few swigs of the tequila, but he hardly appreciated the smooth glide of the liquor down his throat. He was nervous to be there with Brea. Her curly brown hair slightly brushed against his shirt as she leaned towards him to point out an older couple walking down the beach.

"So, what's the farm you're working on?"

"Halimut," he said. She smiled.

"Rose," she said.

"Yeah, I didn't know that was her family when I first met her," he said.

"She's beautiful," Brea said.

"She is, isn't she? She has this weird tough girl act, but her eyes are so soft," he said.

"Wow, make a girl jealous, why don't you?" Brea said. Jacob laughed.

"Okay Yoda," he answered. She punched him on the arm.

As it got darker, Jacob and Brea continued drinking. He briefly remembered having a conversation with Mr. Halimut and Sandra about showing up with a hangover. This made him laugh. And when Brea inquired about what he found amusing, he laughed some more. When she turned to look into his eyes, Jacob proceeded to move her hair out of her face. He was no longer as nervous as he had been earlier.

"She's got nothing on you," he said.

"Who?" Brea asked.

"Rose," he responded.

Thirty minutes later, Jacob had barely opened the door to his room when Brea pushed him onto his bed. She then took off her hat and twirled it at him. Jacob, having consumed most of the tequila in the bottle, was starting to see two of her. He laughed as he moved his head from side to side in an attempt to figure out which one of the two women, he was seeing was the real Brea.

Brea straddled him and kissed him deeply, as though the two of them were paramours reconnecting after a long absence. He could not have planned what was happening. He liked Brea a great deal despite the short time they had known each other and did not think she was open to him due to her quips about his age. *My luck is really turning here.*

"Do you have a condom?' she whispered into his right ear. Her soft slightly slurred voice sent shivers down his spine. He nodded.

"Yes. Yes. I definitely do," he said. She descended and he got up and went into his bathroom to retrieve a condom.

When he returned, Brea was topless on his bed with a seductive look on her face, as though she was trying to trap him in a cage of lustful desires. Jacob's heart beat so fast he thought it would jump out of his chest. He took a deep breath in an attempt to control his body.

"Take your clothes off," she said with a soft yet commanding tone. "You're about to have the best night of your life Mr. Alexander," she added as she began removing her panties.

*

When his eyes opened the following morning, Jacob thought he had dreamed the whole night. The noises she made, the animalistic manner in which she tossed and trashed her body around. He thought it all happened in his mind. That he had concocted this unabashed libertine of a young woman who somehow thought he was attractive. Then he felt her body press against his. And suddenly a rush of blood flowed through his body. It wasn't a dream. It did happen. He smiled.

Brea was still asleep, naked in his bed when Jacob slowly crept out of the bed to take a shower. It was six o'clock. He was expected to be at the Halimut farm at 8 am and did not want to be late. Despite the fact that he hated having to work for Mr. Halimut who by all accounts did not like him, he still thought it would be good to put in some effort to be professional.

"What time is it?" Brea asked as she slowly sat up when he exited the bathroom.

"A little after 6," he said.

"And you're running away?" she asked. He shook his head.

"Technically this is my room, so I'm not running away," he said.

"Did you enjoy yourself last night?" she asked as she grabbed her bikini top and put it on. *How do I answer that without being too enthusiastic?*

"Yeah, you?" he said. She smiled.

"This doesn't have to lead to anything," she said.

"I understand," he said as he walked over to her and kissed her. She chuckled.

"You're cute," she said.

"Dogs are cute, I'm sexy as hell," he said. Brea laughed.

Later in the early afternoon, Luis offered to take Jacob out to lunch to his favorite restaurant in town. It was a small Mexicali place called Mexican Dream. Luis parked his dusty red truck a few blocks down from the restaurant as he did not want to spend half an hour looking for parking in the central area of town. So, they walked down the street, passing an avalanche of young people day drinking as they walked about. Jacob wondered why he wasn't lucky enough to come from a family of wealth. He imagined those young people, who obviously were not in town to work, could depend on their families for sustenance during the summertime, while he had to work in order to fund his drinking.

He had yet to be paid by Mr. Halimut since he just arrived at the farm. He smiled as they passed the bar where Brea worked. He wondered if she was still in his room. When he was leaving earlier, she was still laying in his bed. She promised to lock the door on her way out and thanked him for a fun night.

"Mr. Halimut said he saw you coming out of that bar the other night," Luis said as they waited in line outside of Mexican Dream.

"What is he stalking me?" Jacob asked as he fiddled in his pockets trying to figure out how much money he actually had on him.

"No. I don't think so. I think he likes to drive around with his wife at night sometimes. You know if you ever spend a sober night in this town, you'll notice how clear the night sky is," Luis said. Jacob chuckled.

"That sounds really romantic Luis,"

"Oh, shut up," Luis replied, "Hey look, you see that curly haired woman?" he added as he pointed out a curly haired woman with a tight-fitting outfit with a clipboard in her hands.

"Yeah, who is she?" Jacob asked.

"That's my favorite waitress. Her name is Anselma," Luis said, "This place is the absolute best. All the women are beautiful," he added.

Much to Luis' dismay, Anselma was not their waitress. A young brown-haired woman with a flower tucked in her hair walked Jacob and Luis to their table. *Maya.* She handed both men a menu and told them she would return to get their drink orders. Jacob could hardly contain himself. He was excited about the prospect of interacting with Maya.

"You know they do this to me on purpose," Luis said.

"Do what?"

"They don't give me Anselma because I tip her too well," Luis said. Jacob laughed.

"That's all in your head buddy," Jacob responded.

Through the front window of the Mexican restaurant, Jacob caught sight of Rose who sported a short polka dot dress with navy blue dots. She had her jet-black hair pinned in a bun. She twirled a pen in one hand and held a small notebook in the other. Jacob thought about running out of the restaurant to go talk to her, however, he remembered Luis' warning to stay clear of her so not to jeopardize his job.

"Are you guys ready to order?" Maya said as she returned to the table. Jacob was still looking at Rose who had turned and was looking into the restaurant. *It's as if she could sense that I was looking at her.*

"I'll have the strawberry lemonade," Luis said as he tried to look past Maya to catch a glimpse of Anselma, "Jacob, give her your drink order," Luis added.

"Iced tea, and a little bit of coffee, black, no sugar," Jacob said. Maya wrote the orders down. She seemed to linger. That's what both men thought as her presence got in the way of their sights.

Jacob sat up a little when he noticed Rose walking into the restaurant. He looked to see if she may have been with a companion, but he could not tell if any of the people entering the restaurant at that time were indeed with her. She did not skip a beat and headed straight for Jacob and Luis. Luis looked at Jacob and shook his head. *I didn't even do anything yet.*

"Hey guys!" Rose said as she pulled a chair and sat down.

"Please sit with us," Luis said sarcastically. Rose scoffed.

"Don't be a jerk Luis," she said.

"Hi Rose," Jacob said. Rose smiled at him.

"I didn't get an invite for lunch today," Rose said. Luis chuckled.

"We didn't order our food yet," Jacob said. Luis kicked him under the table. Then Anselma walked by and he quickly turned his attention to the woman with a tray of food in her hands.

"What's his deal?" Rose asked.

"He is in love," Jacob said.

"What about you?" Rose asked.

Maya returned to the table just then, bringing with her the drink orders as well as two glasses of water. She apologized to the group for not having brought Rose a glass of water. She quickly left to get another glass. In the interim, Rose grabbed the iced tea from Jacob's hand, put a straw in it and proceeded to drink from it.

"That's mine," Jacob said. Rose chuckled.

"I know," she said and winked at him. "Luis doesn't like me," she said. Luis scoffed.

"I don't dislike you Rose," Luis said, barely looking in her direction.

"How about you Jacob? Do you dislike me?" she asked as she sucked iced tea through the straw and gulped slowly.

"Umm...I don't really know you," Jacob said.

Maya returned to the table with a glass of water for Rose and proceeded to take their food orders. Jacob sensed the tension at the table. He wondered if what Rose said about Luis disliking her was true. He knew that Luis had a good reason to warn him against engaging in any sort of interaction with Rose. *Did they have a fling? Luis is much older than Rose. She's like a kid compared to him. Maybe she turned him down.*

"Hi Luis," Anselma said as she passed by their table, "I'm going on break. Wanna grab a cigarette?" she added. Luis nodded.

"I'll be back guys. Don't believe anything Rose says," Luis said and left.

Though he decided to heed Luis' warnings, Jacob couldn't help but be curious about the girl whose father was responsible for him being in Greenport. He wondered why she seemed to always be roaming the streets. He grabbed her little notebook and she quickly pulled it back from him.

"What secrets are you hiding in there, Rose?" he asked. She sighed.

"That's none of your business," she said. She pushed the glass of iced tea back to him.

"Hey, you better keep that. I'm not drinking after you," he said. She giggled.

"I don't have anything," she said.

"That's what they all say," he replied.

"Who says that?"

"People who have something," he replied. She chuckled.

Rose excused herself and told him she had to go to the ladies' room. She made sure to grab her pen and little notebook with her. *Maybe she is a drug addict in recovery, and she writes down what she's going through in that book. She is very pretty. But I need this job.* Rose returned almost as quickly as she left the table. She seemed a little giddy.

"Why are you suddenly pumped up?" he asked. She chuckled.

"So, I've decided, I'm going to take you up on your dinner invitation," she said. Jacob smiled.

"I'm sorry," he said. She sat down.

"What do you mean?" she asked.

"Dinner is off the table now, you missed your chance," he said. She was incredulous.

"What? You're turning me down? What are you smoking?" she asked and laughed.

"I'm not allowed to talk to you anymore," he said. He took a sip of his coffee.

"Says who?" she asked. He did not answer. He took another sip of coffee. "Listen contrary to beliefs around here, my father doesn't get to dictate my life Jacob," she added. Again, Jacob took another sip of his coffee.

"What do you write in that thing?" he asked just as Maya returned with a slim young man carrying plates of food.

"Here's your food," Maya said as they placed the food on the table, "did your friend leave?" she added.

"No, he'll be back in a few minutes," Jacob answered. Maya and the young man left.

"Did my dad tell you not to talk to me?" Rose asked. He grabbed a taco off his plate and took a bite out of it all while looking Rose in the eyes. "Don't be a jerk," she said.

Jacob's phone started to ring so he put the taco down and wiped his hand on the napkin next to his plate. Rose rolled her eyes and started eating. When he looked at the phone, he noticed it was Brea calling him. He did not recall giving her his phone number, but he knew anything was possible whenever he was under the influence of alcohol.

"How do you know Brea?" Rose asked as she noticed the number on the phone. Just then Luis walked back into the restaurant. *I slept with her last night.*

"How do you know that's Brea?"

"Jacob, it's a small town," she said. He chuckled.

"I'm famished. We have to get back soon," Luis said as he sat and picked up his burrito.

"We met at the bar the other night," Jacob said. He did not answer the phone.

"Kind of rude not to answer," Rose said, "You're not even old enough to be in a bar. Did she serve you alcohol?" she added. Jacob smirked.

"Are you jealous?" he asked. Luis kicked him under the table again. "ouch...Luis don't worry, I already told young Rose here that I'm not allowed to talk to her," he added. Rose scoffed.

"Luis did you tell him that?" she asked. Luis, his mouth full of food shook his head.

Jacob couldn't help but be gleeful about how bothered Rose was that someone would have told him not to talk to her. He imagined she suspected that her father laid down the law about who was and was not allowed to talk to his daughter as long as they worked for him. He did not think he was the first young man to come work on the farm who would have shown interest in Rose. Afterall, he believed that Rose was an absolute beauty, much like her mother. The two women, he felt, did not fit into the image of homesteaders who maintained farms for family and profit. They seemed like people he knew in his life away from Greenport. They were very much city folks. He wondered if Rose wrote about feeling stuck in Greenport. She had to watch people come and go, including many people her age. Yet she was there, all year long. Jacob felt bad for her. Despite his initial attraction and his desire to get to know her on an intimate level, the threat of her father and the warnings Luis had given him, were enough to dissuade him from making any concerted effort with her. *At least I have Brea.*

A little later, Jacob was back at the farm, and back to painting the barn, a job he found so boring and tedious that he came up with a systematic way of painting which required very little of his brain function. He'd occasionally look at the sheep in the barn and wonder if they were talking about him. His boredom was so intense that he wanted to leave his body and be elsewhere.

He got a signal that his boredom was coming to an end when he saw Rose coming out of the Halimut house with a plate of donuts. She headed straight for Jacob. Jacob cursed his luck. It was one thing to talk with Rose and flirt with her away from the farm, but he knew better than to engage with her on the farm. He had gotten enough warnings to know that it was a serious matter. She stopped on the edge of the tarp and waited for him to turn around. He did not want to turn. But he didn't want to offend her either. In his experience, offending a beautiful girl did not always work out.

"Hi Rose," he said.

"Took you awhile to turn around," she said, "I know you saw me coming out of the house," she added. He chuckled.

"I don't eat donuts," he said. She scoffed.

"You're a liar. Everyone likes donuts. Plus, I made these from scratch," she said.

"Even more reason for me not to eat it," he said and chuckled.

"Don't be a jerk," Rose said and handed him the plate. Jacob grabbed a donut from the plate, and she watched as he took a bite out of it.

"Mmm" he said, "tastes good," he added.

"Of course, it does," she said with a smile. Jacob put down the brushes and walked over the tarp to a stack of hay behind him and sat down. Rose sat next to him.

"You didn't bring me anything to drink," he said.

"I'm not your servant,"

"Not, yet," he said. She hit his arm. She put the plate down next to her.

"I like you Jacob," she said. Jacob laughed. "It's not funny. I'm being honest with you," she added.

"Rose. You're beautiful. And I think you are supercool,"

"It's because of my dad, isn't it?" she asked.

"I came here to work, and he holds all the power...I like you too but..." he said. Rose leaned towards him and kissed him. Jacob pulled back.

"You have soft lips for a boy," she said.

"You can't do that Rose. I don't want to cause any problems here," he said.

"If you are afraid of my dad then there's really nothing interesting about you after all. Oh well, I thought you were one of those strong driven types," she said. He smirked. She was trying to get under his skin. Jacob leaned towards her and kissed her. Then he pulled back again.

"You have no idea what you're getting yourself into Rose," he said and got up.

Rose also got up. Jacob finished eating the donut he had in his hand. He then wiped his hands on his jeans. Rose laughed. He could tell that she liked him. As he looked into her eyes, he thought about the fact that it would not be long before he got fired. Rose was trouble, even if she didn't mean to be. Even if she had no control over her father's behavior, his influence on her life was going to be prevalent. She stepped closer to him and kissed him again. Jacob licked his lips and then gently touched hers.

"You have hard lips for a girl," he said. She laughed.

"You're a jerk," she said.

"I know," he replied. "I have to return to my wonderful painting job," he added.

"What are you doing later?" she asked.

"Probably drinking...what else is there to do in this place?"

"With Brea?" she asked. He chuckled.

"Bye Rose," he said and walked back over the tarp.

Rose grabbed her plate of donuts and headed back to the house. Jacob felt all giddy inside. Despite the fact that he had been with other girls, he had this inkling that there was something pure and light about Rose. She seemed to be able to command her space, despite the fact that she lived under her father's thumb. He knew it was risky to get involved with her. But this was part of why he came to Greenport for the summer. He wanted to enjoy himself and explore his desires.

At the end of the working day, Jacob was putting his tools away along with Luis when Mr. Halimut drove up to them in his Jeep. He put his car in park but left the engine running. He descended and walked over to Jacob and Luis.

"Jacob come take a drive with me. I'll drop you off," Mr. Halimut said.

"Oh, that's okay, I'm going to hang out with Luis in town for a little bit," Jacob said. Mr. Halimut smirked.

"I insist. I can drop you off wherever you and Luis are meeting," Mr. Halimut said. Jacob glanced at Luis who had a telling smirk on his face. *God, I'm about to get fired already?*

"Sure," Jacob said and grabbed his bag. He followed Mr. Halimut into the Jeep.

Five minutes into the drive, Mr. Halimut still had not said a word to Jacob. He turned the radio onto the local easy listening channel and drove, occasionally humming to a tune. Jacob, the discomfort overtaking his body, cast his eyes outside the car window, watching as they passed luscious green fields. Jacob occasionally checked his phone, hoping he'd get a phone call to break the monotony of this dreadful drive with his boss.

"It's beautiful out here," Jacob said. He suspected Mr. Halimut was not going to say a word. And Jacob could no longer handle the silence in the car. Mr. Halimut grunted. *That's not much of an answer.* "Did you grow up in this town like Rose?" Jacob added.

"I need you to stop talking to my daughter," Mr. Halimut said. His tone was serious.

"Umm...I"

"I saw what happened between you two earlier by the barn," Mr. Halimut said. *Gee, you don't do any work around this place other than spy on your daughter?*

"Look Mr. Halimut, I told Rose I wasn't allowed to talk to her anymore. She came onto me," Jacob said. Mr. Halimut smirked.

"Jacob, I know my daughter. She does these things to get under my skin. She's really good at it. So, I'm telling you, if you want to continue working for me, you'll stay clear of her."

"With all due respect, Rose is her own person. I can't help it if she comes to talk to me. I've tried to be respectful. I made it clear to her..." Jacob said but the car stopped abruptly. He hadn't noticed, but Mr. Halimut drove him to the Inn. Mr. Hagen was sitting outside in khaki shorts and a short-sleeved dress shirt. He waved at Jacob.

"See you," Mr. Halimut said. Jacob grabbed his bag and got out of the car. Mr. Halimut drove off.

CHAPTER 3

The following week, Jacob found himself trapped in a forest. He did not remember how he got into the forest. All he remembered was that he had finally finished the work that was assigned to him, which consisted of planting flowers on the edges of the farm. He had returned to the barn which was the bane of his existence while at the same time providing a sort of familiarity that he could hang onto. Then he found himself in a forest.

For some odd reason, as he was trying to find his way through this strange forest, a river, or more precisely, a body of water ran through the forest. On one side of the body of water, was Brea, in a beautiful short burgundy dress, her eyes sparkling under the mid-afternoon sunlight and her skin, a delicious golden color from having been in the sun for a while.

On the other side of the water, was Rose, in a cream-colored dress that hugged her buddy and ran down to her ankle. She wore a white hat to block the sun from her eyes. These two women did not say a word to him. They motioned for him to come to them. Jacob smacked himself a few times, trying to make sense of what he was seeing. He knew on some level that what he was seeing could not be real. It would be impossible for a body of water to emerge in a forest. It was even more strange to think that somehow Brea and Rose would appear out of nowhere to beckon him to them.

This isn't real. Did I do some drugs and didn't know about it? Maybe Luis put something in my water bottle. This isn't happening. Maybe it's a sign. My mind is sending me a message. I'm starting to find myself between these two women. Well girls, really. Rose is young. She's only a year younger than me, but still. That's young. But Brea, she's so self-assured. She knows what she wants. She's grown. She can take charge.

He smacked himself again a few times. However, the scene he found himself in did not change. Brea and Rose were still there. The body of water was still there. He waved at them, and they each continued to motion for him to come closer to them.

"Where are we? Is this real?" he said aloud. They did not answer.

I'm going crazy. Maybe all the drinking I've been doing has not been good for me. Maybe I need to stop drinking. This is a dream. This must be a dream. I just need to wake up out of it before I start conjuring up some weird things. God they're so beautiful. What a lucky guy Jacob.

He looked at the body of water and noticed how still it was. So he walked closer, ignoring the women and their motions. He touched the water. It felt warm, unlike any body of water he had been in. So, Jacob decided that if this truly was a dream he was experiencing, it would be best to do something unusual. He walked right into the water.

When the sunlight broke through and touched his eyes, Jacob moved his body back a little as if he was going to be hit with something. Then he finally fully opened his eyes. He had a pounding headache. His breathing was labored as he struggled to catch his breath. It was as if he had been drowning.

"Are you okay," a female voice said. He turned to look. It was Sandra.

"I just had the weirdest dream," he answered. He was startled to see her there.

Jacob shook his arms as the sharp pain in his head intensified with the bright sun hitting his eyes. He tried to stand up but Sandra motioned for him to stay down. She had a bright smile on her face as she tucked her hair behind her ears. Next to her was a digital camera. Jacob's heart raced as he looked at the beautiful woman sitting on the grass across from him.

"I was watching you sleep," she said. Jacob cleared his throat. *That's not weird at all.*

"Oh,"

"You looked like you were having a battle in your sleep," she said and chuckled.

"Ah," he said. He could hardly formulate words. He was stumped. Jacob never struggled for words like that before. Now he found himself possessed. He found her beauty frightening, and the fact that she was much older than him, enthralling.

"What?" she said.

"Huh?"

"You're staring at me. A lot," she said.

"Oh," he said. He hadn't realized that his eyes barely left her face since he woke up from his nightmare of a nap. "Does that make you uncomfortable?" he asked. *Be cool Jacob.*

"No, that doesn't make me uncomfortable," she said. She stared into his eyes, as if she was trying to push him beyond his comfort zone. He assumed she probably felt that due to his age, he would not know how to handle being around an older woman.

Sandra sat up a little bit, her breasts protruding more than before. Jacob instinctively licked his lips. Then he wondered if his action was too obvious. He knew that despite being married, Sandra must have to fight off men for whom her beauty was intoxicating. He wiped his eyes. *Maybe this is all just part of my dream.* He hadn't noticed that her light blue shirt was slightly see-through. He could see her black bra. *Control yourself. Don't say anything stupid to this woman.* He never had to think that much when talking to girls his age. Something about Sandra made him scared. Almost as if he would be punished if he didn't pay her the utmost respect.

"Jacob," she said. He blinked excessively.

"Umm...yeah?" he answered. He cleared his throat. "I need something to drink," he added.

"Can I take your picture?" she asked. *She wants to take my picture? Looking like this? All sweaty?*

"Uh...yeah, that's fine," he said. The words barely made it out of his mouth when she started clicking away. Jacob did not have the opportunity to strike a pose. "Should I..."

"No, that's not necessary. Just stay the way you are. I like taking candid shots. Poses are for models," she said.

"Are you saying I'm not good looking enough to be a model Mrs. Halimut?" he asked. She laughed.

"Oh, you're precious," she said, "would you like to come in for some cake?" she added as she stood up.

How could he say no? He wondered. He was curious about what the Halimut house looked like inside. And a part of him hoped that he'd also run into Rose while in the house to get a sense of what her life was really like.

Jacob stood up slowly and followed behind Sandra as they walked to the Halimut house. From the outside it looked like a big house. Mr. Halimut had a strict rule about his workers not entering his house. He was adamant about not mixing his work life with his private life. Most of the workers suspected he did not want these unruly men -and they were mostly men who worked on the farm - around his wife and his daughter. Despite his desire to keep his workers at a distance, Mr. Halimut could not stop his wife and daughter from inviting the workers to the house. Sometimes the workers would be invited to come in for dinner, or for a drink. Mr. Halimut was careful about not making anyone who was invited to the house feel uncomfortable about being there. Though he was clear that if any of them made an advance on his wife or his daughter, they'd find themselves unemployed.

So, it was with some trepidation that Jacob entered the Halimut house. He had to toe the line carefully. The foyer of the house was big with a bench on each side. Jacob removed his shoes so as not to get the house dirty. Sandra did the same. He noticed her toenails were painted purple. She motioned for him to follow her into the kitchen. On the way, they crossed the large living room with two oversized couches and a mid-sized love chair.

The kitchen, with its walls painted crisp white, smelled like cake. On top of the large farm-style island, was a big round red velvet cake. Jacob took in a deep breath. His lungs filled with the scent of the cake. Suddenly his body registered hunger. His stomach growled as he watched Sandra elegantly walk behind the island. She seemed to glide. He could barely hear her footsteps.

"I baked it this morning," she said, "The icing should be perfect right about now," she added as she reached inside the cabinets to the right of the marble sink. Jacob, uncontrollably aroused by the older woman in front of him, intuitively licked his lips as he watched her grab two small plates.

"You...you have a nice house," he said as he moved closer to the island, as a way to hide his erection.

"Thanks Jacob," she said, "has anyone ever called you Jake?" she asked as she opened a drawer to her left and unearthed a knife.

"No, no. No one calls me Jake. I've always been Jacob," he replied. She dug the knife into the red velvet cake and sliced it.

"Jacob is a nice name," she said, "here," she added as she handed him a big piece of cake.

"wow, that's a big piece of cake," he said, "thank you," he added.

"I'm sure you can handle it," she said, "a big growing boy like you needs to eat more," she added. She smiled and watched as he put a piece of the cake in his mouth.

"Mmm, that's delicious," he said, "are you not having any Mrs. Halimut?" he added. She smirked.

"Call me Sandra," she said as she cut another piece of cake.

Sandra. What a beautiful name. It flows through my mouth just like this piece of cake. God this cake is good. I wonder if she put something special in it to make it so...moist. What am I doing here? If that man sees me in his house, I may have more than just my job to lose. Why are some men so obsessive over their women? I mean, he should be confident that... He noticed that she was staring at him while simultaneously putting a piece of cake in her mouth. It was as if she knew every inch of the kitchen and could move about without paying attention to what she was doing.

Sandra's seeming interest in the young man startled him a bit. He did not know what to do with her attention. Were he around Brea or Rose, he'd know exactly how to behave. He'd know what to say to those young women to convey his interest, or at the minimum, feign his surprise that they're interested in him at all. Sandra made him nervous. The fact that she did not seem to care that she was married put him on edge a little, but he found it all the while intoxicating.

"Um...did you always want to do this?" he asked. *That's not even a clear question. How is she supposed to answer that question?*

Sandra put her fork down next to her half-eaten piece of cake. She opened the window above the sink and a flow of warm air came into the room. Then he watched attentively as she walked over to the oversized metallic grey refrigerator and brought out a pitcher of lemonade. Jacob gulped. He hadn't realized he was thirsty. In fact, he could not really tell whether he was thirsty or not. The signal was there, and his body was reacting to it.

"Did I always want to do what?" she asked as she placed the pitcher on the kitchen island, "Jacob will you do me a favor and grab two tall glasses from that cabinet behind you?" she added. He nodded.

"I meant, live and work on the farm," Jacob said as he grabbed two glasses from the cabinet she pointed at. Sandra scoffed. There was a tone of annoyance in her voice. Though when he turned around, she was still smiling. She was still, as though she hadn't moved a muscle.

"Did I always want to live in this little coastal town where everyone knows everyone's business and have to deal with the smell of cow manure all day?" she asked. Jacob chuckled. "No, this wasn't part of any plan. This was my husband's life...still is," she said as he handed her the glasses. She poured lemonade into each glass.

"So... delicious," he said as he took a sip of lemonade. "What did you do before all this?" he asked. Sandra held the glass of lemonade to her lips, contemplating his question. Her eyes lingered. Jacob felt like a prey being studied, to be hunted.

"I used to be a lawyer. Most of my clients were politicians," she said. Jacob was dumbfounded.

She must be bored out of her mind to be stuck here, doing this. Making cakes and lemonade when she has a brain to be doing something else. Jacob wanted to ask her why she would give up a life practicing law and rubbing shoulders with politicians and businessmen so that she could come work on a farm with her husband. However, he feared he'd be insulting her by suggesting the life she was now living was somehow inferior to the life she lived in the past.

"We moved here mostly because my husband thought it would be better for Rose. she wasn't sleeping well when we lived in the city. Out here, it's quieter and... life is simpler," she said.

What a drag. She doesn't want to be here. There was a fire in Sandra, however dim the flames may be, Jacob could pick it up in her. She wasn't meant for this kind of life. He felt sorry for her, that she had to be stuck with a husband who would upend her life the way he had. As for Rose, Jacob wondered if the young woman herself was happy to be in Greenport. It was a nice town, but he couldn't imagine there was much to do for most of the year bar the summertime when the town was suddenly filled with people, young and old.

"Do you miss it?" he asked. She nodded. She did not need to think about it.

"I occasionally call my old team and listen to salacious rumors about their clients," she said. She had a wide smile on her face. There was a new kind of warmth emanating from her. "What about you? What are your plans for when you finish school?" she added.

His plans? He hadn't thought about that. Jacob scarcely thought about what he would do in the future. He planned on going off to business school. He knew he'd end up in an office somewhere, doing something. What exactly that is, he never thought much about. In some ways, Jacob did not care too much about the future. He had no desires beyond that which can be satisfied by a human body. He scratched his head.

"I don't know...I'll probably go to business school or something," he said.

"Hmm,"

"What?"

"You seem like such a bright young man. I think there is so much you can do with your life," she said. He shrugged.

"I guess..." he said, "sometimes having so many choices can be part of the problem," he added. She chuckled.

"Young people usually feel like they know exactly how their lives are going to turn out," she said.

"I'm a special breed," he said. *Ooh, that was a nice touch. I'm back in the game baby!*

"I can see that," she said and laughed. "You know my daughter..."

"I've stayed clear of her. I'm not looking for trouble," he interjected. She laughed.

"Jacob, has it occurred to you that maybe women are the ones looking for trouble?" she said. He was silent.

What does she mean by that? Maybe she's looking for trouble. No that can't be. She's much older than me. That's...no i don't think that's in the cards. He looked at his wristwatch. He should get back to work. Mr. Halimut would not be happy to find him in the house eating his cake and drinking his lemonade. The thought of those two things made Jacob smile. Though he was adamant about not wanting trouble, a part of him found joy in the idea that he could be doing something that would unravel the life of the tightly wound Mr. Halimut.

"What I mean by that is that I think she is a little too inexperienced for a vibrant young man like you," she said.

"I uh"

"Have you ever been with an older woman?" she asked.

This is a trick question. Is she coming on to me or is this all in my head? Why would she sideline her own daughter like that? This woman is more trouble than I imagined. I kind of like this. Is that wrong? To be into a married woman. Knowing that there is no chance of this coming to anything. His hesitation to answer her made her chuckle. She cut him another slice of cake, and Jacob dutifully ate it, all the while leaving her question unanswered.

When he finished the second piece of cake, she poured him more lemonade. It was as though she was training him to respond to her cues. Jacob realized what was happening. He was being sucked into this woman's world, eagerly responding to her prompts though no words were being exchanged between them. The way she stared at him made him uneasy, as though he was doing something wrong. Despite his attempts to look away from her, Sandra persisted with her disarming gaze. He could do nothing. He had no defense for the charms of this experienced woman who looked as though she was cross-examining him with every subtle movement.

He knew then that Sandra was right when she said her daughter was inexperienced. Whatever he might have felt in Rose's presence, did not compare to what he was feeling there in the kitchen. He was grateful to have the island separating them, so not to give away the fact that he was aroused beyond control.

"I... I should get back to work," he finally said. She smiled.

"You didn't answer my question Jacob," she said. She dragged out his name a little. *My God, I'm going to tear my pants up if I stay here longer. This woman is crazy hot, and she knows how to toy with me. She knows I'm uncomfortable.*

"I've been with women of different experiences," he said. She covered the cake with the plastic lid.

"There are certain things that you only learn from experience. True experience. Openness, uninhibited...lust," she said.

"Mrs. Halimut, you don't understand, I think you are crazy hot and I can't tell you how many dirty thoughts have run through my mind already, but you are a married woman and I don't think this sort of conversation is appropriate," he said. She chuckled. *Oh, you idiot. She's laughing at you. You've finally made a fool of yourself.*

"I told you to stop calling me that Jacob," she said with a serious face.

Jacob could not ascertain whether she was upset with him or not. Her face was still, calculating. It once again had the essence of a predator stalking its prey. This energized Jacob. He enjoyed the idea of an older woman luring him. It validated his own ideas about being desirable.

He decided to walk over to her side of the island and show her just how much he desired her. He was not going to hold back. He certainly was not going to continue being respectful now that she had shown him how easily she was willing to broach the subject of his dalliances with older women. Then he heard the footsteps. They were the steps of well-worn boots with swathes of sand and rocks stuck within the wedges at the bottom.

Jacob stopped mid-stride as he listened for the shoes. Sandra, recognizing that her husband's footsteps had stopped the young man who was on his way to turn the tables on her, flashed a smile. It was a beautiful smile, but one meant to disguise disappointment. This was not what she wanted. Jacob was not sure if he had just been rescued or derailed. The scent of musty cigars soon flowed into the room, overtaking that of the wonderful red velvet cake he had just eaten.

"Oh, Jacob, here you are," Mr. Halimut said, "keeping my wife entertained?" he added as he walked over to Sandra and kissed her on the cheek. *A kiss on the cheek? What a travesty. If that was my wife, I wouldn't spare a moment. I'd be giving her deep kisses every chance I got. What a loser.*

"She told me she made some world class cakes, and I just had to come try some," Jacob said.

"And?" Sandra asked.

"You weren't lying," Jacob said, "Mr. Halimut, you are one lucky man," Jacob said. He did his best not to look Sandra in the eyes. He did not want Mr. Halimut to catch on.

"I really am. How about you? Any young ladies keeping you busy and distracted?" Mr. Halimut said. Jacob laughed.

"Yeah, there's one that I'm fond of," Jacob said.

"Nice," Mr. Halimut said.

"I hope you're being a perfect gentleman," Sandra said as she leaned onto Mr. Halimut's shoulder.

"My mother would expect nothing less," Jacob said. Mr. Halimut chuckled.

Jacob would have run out of there if he thought it wouldn't look suspicious. Despite the fact that he hadn't done anything wrong, something in him felt wrong, yet delectable. He enjoyed the fact that Sandra flirted with him. He pushed his plate in Sandra's direction and grabbed a napkin from the holder next to the cake and wiped his mouth.

"So, what are your plans when you are done with school?" Mr. Halimut asked.

"Not farming," Jacob said. They all laughed. "I'm sorry I don't mean it like that," he added. Mr. Halimut chuckled.

"It's perfectly fine Jacob. This life is not for everyone," Mr. Halimut said. *You have no idea. Your wife, your life partner doesn't want this life. But you're too blind to see that. I don't get why she doesn't just tell him.*

The farm life was not for Jacob. He knew that before coming to Greenport. There was no part of him that was under the illusion that he'd like to someday be a farmer. Jacob was interested in learning. And working on the farm was just another piece of that process. It also did not hurt that being in this small beach town helped his prospects in terms of summer flings, a goal much more aligned with his sensibilities.

"But it is important for a young man like you to have a plan in place and to go through with it," Mr. Halimut said.

"Thank you for the cake and lemonade Sandra," Jacob said, finally making eye contact with the woman.

"Anytime dear. You are always welcome here," she said. He smiled.

As he exited the house, he heard a set of footsteps coming down the stairs. Jacob wanted to get away from the house as fast as possible. He found his conversation with Sandra thrilling, and was still trying to bring himself back down to earth as the erection in his pants persisted. Then he smelled the rosemary-tinged perfume. He knew it was Rose. He continued walking as he did not want Mr. Halimut to see him talking to his daughter. *It's enough that he almost caught me with his wife. This family is really something else.* He sped up his walking and she picked up her pace right along.

"Why are you running away from me?" Rose asked as they reached the barn, he spent days painting.

"I'm not running away from you," he said. She did not have a happy look on her face. She looked as though she was upset about something or with someone.

"Do you like me?" she asked. *Is this middle school all over again?*

"What kind of question is that?" he responded. She had a blue pen in her hand and began twirling it around her slim fingers.

"Do you like me or not?" she asked. Jacob sighed. *Sandra was right. Her daughter is a little immature. Who cares about whether they're liked or not?*

"Rose…"

"I've been hearing things about you and Brea," she said.

"We are not in middle school. If there is something you want to say to me just come out and say it," he said.

"You know she sleeps around," Rose said. Jacob smirked. "I think you're a really nice guy. And…do you like her?" she added.

Jacob was dumbfounded. While he had done his share of flirting with Rose, he never got the impression that she took him seriously or that she would have developed feelings for him in such a short time. He did like Brea. In fact, he was falling more and more for Brea every time he saw her. He hadn't considered that Rose, who had until then brushed aside most of his advances, was becoming fond of him. *I'd only break her heart. How can she not see that?*

"I like a lot of people Rose," he said.

"That's a cop-out," she said, "I'd be very careful around my mother if I were you. She's an incredibly miserable person," she added. Jacob chuckled. He walked up to Rose, grabbed her face in his hands and kissed her.

"You people are absolutely nuts," he said. He turned and walked away, not giving her a chance to process what he had just done or to react to it.

CHAPTER 4

The two Saturdays later, Jacob was beckoned to the pub by Luis. He was told to meet outside at 7 pm to start the night off right. Jacob had hoped to spend the night with Brea, however she had not been returning his calls after several attempts. Jacob was more than happy to leave her alone. That was until he received the call from Luis to meet at Limerick, the bar where she worked. Saturdays were one of the days when Brea made the most money at the bar. Jacob knew that. So, he knew he'd better not bother her while she was working.

As he walked down the street a block from the bar, he noticed Luis walking up to the bar from the opposite direction with two men around his age. One was a dark-skinned black man in a panama hat wearing shorts that were made out of cut up jeans. The other was a brown-haired man whose hair dropped down to his shoulders.

Jacob waved at the men, then he quickly lowered his arm, in an attempt not to look too eager to have friends. Luis embraced Jacob as if he was a long-lost friend. Jacob was not used to this sort of affectionate reaction from other men. He hugged Luis back, so not to communicate that he somehow had an issue with being hugged. Luis introduced the two men.

"This is my friend Liam," Luis said as he grabbed the long-haired man by the shoulder, "he's from Idaho," he added. Liam laughed.

"Yeah man," Liam said.

"Far from home," Jacob said.

"Aren't we all?" Liam responded.

"And this beautiful jerk over here is my friend Freddy," Luis said as he pulled the black man closer to him, "we've been friends since first grade," he added.

"I keep trying to get away from this guy," Freddy said, "nice to meet you Jacob, let's drink huh?" he added. Jacob nodded.

The bar was full of people and noise as the men entered. Jacob marveled at the number of young women, presumably college students, that were in the establishment with a drink in hand, bodies swaying to the music blasting from the speakers.

He followed Luis and the other men as they walked over to a corner of the bar with a little bit of space. Once there, Luis alerted the man standing behind the bar that they were ready to drink. The man glanced at him and nodded. *They must know each other.*

Jacob scoured the room for Brea. He hated being out without her. Despite the fact that the two of them had not promised one another exclusivity, he was fond of her. He enjoyed her not so funny jokes and the way she batted away his adoration. When he thought he might have finally seen her amidst the crowd of people in the bar, Luis tapped him on the shoulder. There was a line of tequila shots and mugs filled to the brim with beer behind them.

"Let's go boy, don't be a wimp," Luis said. All the men grabbed their shot glasses. Jacob looked behind him, trying to see if Brea had seen him, or if that was Brea, he had seen in the first place. "Let's go Jacob! Drink up!" Luis added. Jacob took the shot.

A few minutes later, Jacob finally laid eyes on Brea. He was three drinks in at that point. He looked around him. He couldn't understand how Luis and the other men were able to drink so much, so quickly. He did not want to look weak in front of them, so when they ordered another round, he enthusiastically accepted the invitation to drink.

Brea was on her way to the back of the bar when Jacob hurried away from his group to catch up with her. A group of young women, evidently drunk and struggling to keep one another afoot, slowed down his progress. He managed to weave his way around them, avoiding shouts of "hey blonde guy!" as he chased after Brea who barely noticed that he had been trying to get her attention.

"Hey!" he shouted as she opened the door to the back. She turned and noticed that it was Jacob. She had a frown on her face. She continued her walk and he followed after her to the back. Jacob grabbed her arm as they stepped out.

"Let go of me!" she shouted. Her rage seemed sudden and uncalled for. Jacob was confused.

"Hey, is everything okay?"

"She said to let go of her, are you deaf?" a man with a deep voice said behind Jacob. Jacob thought to turn and tell the man to mind his own business. However, when he turned around, he noticed that the man was twice his size. He quickly let go of Brea.

"River, it's okay. I can handle this," Brea said. The man grunted, lit a cigarette, and walked by Jacob, shooting him a discerning look as he walked on.

"What is there to handle?" Jacob asked. Brea scoffed. She walked over to the fence behind the bar and leaned against it, facing him for the first time that afternoon. "Listen I just wanted to know if you wanted to hang out tonight after you're done here. That's all. If you don't want to you can say no, you're not my..." Jacob said.

"You know, I'd really appreciate it if you'd keep your girlfriend away from me," Brea said. Jacob was dumbfounded. *Girlfriend?*

"What are you talking about?"

"Your friend Rose ambushed me and my friends at the beach today asking that we leave you alone. I know you're a little young and you may not know how to handle things, but I don't have time for these childish confrontations," she said.

"First of all, you're only a few years older than me. Second, Rose is not my girlfriend. I don't know what she said to you or what she has in her head but there's nothing there," Jacob said. Brea chuckled.

"She sure as hell doesn't know that. Maybe you should stop leading her on," Brea said, Jacob shook his head.

"Hey what the hell are you doing out here man? Let's drink!" Luis said as he opened the door.

"Yeah I'll be in in a second," Jacob said, "you know, for all your maturity, you didn't think to come talk to me about whatever it is that Rose said to you. And I'm the bad guy in all of this right?" he said to Brea.

"I don't need..."

"Enjoy the rest of your day Brea," Jacob said and abruptly entered the bar.

Jacob prepared himself for what he knew was going to come next. As he walked back to the front of the bar where he left his group, he could see them whispering amongst one another. This was nothing new. This was a tried and true practice among men, and he knew he'd have to endure. Enduring the torture of being ridiculed by other men was common. He'd have done it to others in the past, and he was no stranger to being the receiver.

"Did your girlfriend give you permission to come drink with the big boys?" Freddy asked and ran his hand through Jacob's hair. Jacob laughed.

"She's not my girlfriend," Jacob replied. Luis smirked. He slid Jacob a shot of Tequila.

"You guys should have seen the look on her face. It was like a mom yelling at her kid. It was precious. And little Jacob just stood there, being told what to do." Luis said. Jacob scoffed and took the shot of Tequila.

"Ha-ha, you guys are so funny," Jacob said.

"Listen man, it happens to all of us. We are trapped by the beauty of women. Can you imagine if all women were ugly? Like really hideous. None of us would stand there and listen to the nonsense they have to say," Liam said. A group of women nearby started shouting at Liam in Portuguese. The long-haired man simply shrugged.

"I think you've offended them," Jacob said as he drank from the tall glass of beer.

"Oh well, women are always offended," Liam said, "you have catching up to do buddy," he added.

A few hours later, Jacob was standing outside the bar with Luis while he smoked when his phone started to ring. He looked at the phone but didn't immediately recognize the number, so he ignored it. Luis, with the cigarette between his lips, struggled to keep himself up. *And he thought he could out-drink me? Lightweight.*

Jacob's phone buzzed. He thought it was a phone call but then noticed it was a text message. When he opened the message, he quickly turned his phone a little so that Luis would not see the message he received. It was a message from Sandra Halimut. Jacob, his eyes creating multiples of everything he looked at, was excited to see that Sandra was inviting him to come to the Halimut house. It did not occur to him to ask her whether her husband was at home or to inquire about why she was asking him to come to the house. All he knew was that he had been invited and he did not want to disappoint her.

"Hey, I have to get going," Jacob said, Luis laughed.

"No, you don't. We still have some more drinking to do. Don't be a punk," Luis said as he took one last drag of his cigarette.

"No, I really have to get going. And you can't even keep up with me anyway," Jacob said. Luis laughed.

"You're right. You're better at handling your liquor than I am," Luis said.

"I have alcoholics in my family. It's a sort of genetic lottery," Jacob said. He rubbed his eyes to try and gain some focus.

"That is a weird thing to be proud of," Luis said. Jacob chuckled.

Jacob called a cab and then helped Luis get back into the bar. He stood outside and waited for a few minutes for the cab. And as he browsed through messages on his phone, Brea came out of the bar. She tossed her curly hair behind her and fixed her eyes on him. It was as if she came out specifically to talk to him. He looked at the time on his phone. *The cab should be here soon.*

"You owe me an apology," she said. She smelled like the beach. He took a deep breath, taking in the smells of the salt from the water.

"I don't owe you anything," he said as the cab pulled in front of the bar. Brea's jaw dropped.

"So, you're just going to be a jerk?" she asked. She reached and grabbed his arm as he moved towards the cab.

"If that's what you decided I am, then there's nothing I can do about it," he said. He released her hand from his arm and entered the cab.

Jacob knew that Brea would be incensed by his behavior towards her. He wanted her to be upset with him. The last thing he wanted was for her to think that she could dictate how he behaved. He was annoyed that she was upset with him regarding Rose but didn't think to come to him to find out what the deal was between them. He would have told her the truth. He would have told her that there was nothing between them. He would have told her about Rose's sudden infatuation with him. But she didn't ask. She assumed. And that annoyed him.

"We're here," the driver said as he pulled in front of the Halimut farmhouse.

"Oh, that was fast," Jacob said.

"Small town," the driver responded. Jacob paid the man and left the car. He was still a little drunk, so he took deep breaths on intervals as he walked to the front door.

The front door opened just as Jacob was about to knock. On the other side was Sandra Halimut in a long dress with flower patterns. He could see, though he hardly believed what his eyes showed him, that she was not wearing a bra. She smiled at him and motioned for him to enter. Jacob carefully walked into the house, looking around to see if anyone else was there. *This must be some kind of trick. I'm going to get in here and they're going to murder me. I'm sure I've seen this scene in a movie somewhere.*

Jacob stumbled and fell to the ground as he followed her into the living room. Embarrassed, he sat on the floor for a few moments. Sandra stood by and watched him, with a smirk on her face. It was clear to him that she took pleasure out of seeing him struggle. When he managed to get up, he took his shoes off.

"Where is Mr. Halimut tonight?" he asked her.

"Come into the kitchen," she said, "I baked a new cake tonight and I wanted to give you a taste," she added. He followed her into the kitchen.

"Smells good," Jacob said.

"Rose and her father went into New York City for a show. They won't be back for a while," she said as she cut into the cake, "it's apple crumb cake," she added.

"You didn't want to go?" Jacob asked. Sandra walked over to the coffee pot to her right and poured coffee into a mug and handed it to him along with the cake.

"Are you going to spend all night asking me about my husband?" Sandra asked as Jacob took a sip of the coffee. He coughed.

Sandra watched as he ate the cake. He thought she'd say something, anything, to break the silence, but she did not. She stood there, watching him, as if trying to figure out a way to unlock a gem. So, Jacob ate the cake and drank the coffee. *She is one weird lady. Why won't she say something?*

"Umm, it's..."

"Shh, don't ruin a perfectly good silent moment," Sandra interjected, "people underestimate the power of non-verbal communication. You don't always have to talk," she added.

Jacob continued to take small bites of the delectable crumb cake as the woman of the house watched him. He could tell she derived pleasure from observing him. She licked her lips as he licked a piece of cake off the side of his mouth. Then he watched as she dragged her finger across the kitchen counter in a slow back and forth manner.

"Good?" she asked. He nodded.

"Very. You're...a skilled woman," he said. She smiled.

"You're a very good boy," she said.

Jacob grabbed the plate and walked around the island to the sink, all the while fixing his gaze on her. He was prepared to play her game. He was more sober than he had been when he first entered the house. He could smell her lilac scented perfume as he stood behind her washing his plate. He thought she'd move when his buttocks touched hers, but she did not move.

"You don't have to wash the plate," she said.

"Mrs. Halimut, it would be rude of me to eat your delicious cake and leave the plate in the sink," Jacob said.

"I thought I told you not to call me that?" she said. Jacob turned around, now facing her back.

He moved an inch forward, pressing his groin against her back. Sandra quivered. Jacob smiled when she turned her head a little to look at him. *What the hell am I doing?* He reached out and touched her hand with his right hand and traced the lines on her hand.

"Why don't you leave if you're unhappy?" he asked. She scoffed.

"Who said I was unhappy?" she responded. He chuckled.

"Well I'm all sorts of confused then," Jacob said. He took in a deep breath next to her ear and then blew air into it. Sandra quivered again.

"A woman doesn't necessarily need her husband to make her happy," she said. "All men have a role to play," she added.

I'm definitely going to get fired. This woman is insane. And sexy. God she is sexy. Stay cool. She turned around, as if she could read his mind. Jacob was frozen, though he managed to hide the fact that he was terrified of what was going on at that moment. He had never been with an older woman before. He certainly had not been with a married woman before. This was new territory for him. And it was terrifying, and rightly so.

Sandra stared into his eyes, and Jacob did not blink. It was difficult. It would have been easy to send his eyes fluttering, looking in any direction but her eyes. Yet he maintained his gaze, to match her energy. Then she inched forward a little, their bodies fully touching one another. Even if he wanted to, he could not hide the erection pulsing in his pants. He wondered if she was as aroused as he was. The atmosphere was charged.

What was once a space filled with the powerful scents of cake and coffee, was suddenly filled with the intoxicating scent of a woman fully in charge of her subject. And he was every bit her subject. He knew he had no control, no say on the matter. Sandra did not flinch. It was for him, an education in control.

When she finally kissed him, he got pulled further into her world. Jacob couldn't help it. He could feel that his briefs were a little wet. He wondered if she knew. *There's no way she would know. She can't tell. At least I got that one out of the way.* He kissed her back, pulling her soft lips into his. She closed her eyes, and he closed his eyes. For a moment, the two of them traveled into a world where their bodies were the only things that mattered. Though the wind blew through the open windows, Jacob barely felt it. All he could feel was her warm body touching his. *Are my clothes still on? What is happening right now?*

When he finally opened his eyes, she was looking at him. Then she smirked as she pushed her hands under his shirt, feeling his body. Jacob pushed forward a little, pushing her against the kitchen counter. Then, as if being controlled by a force other than his mind, he lifted one of her legs up with his hand, sliding his hand towards her butt in the process. *She's not wearing any panties. Oh God, I'm going to be in so much trouble.*

"What if he walks in now?" Jacob asked. *Why are you asking such a stupid question right now? Why now? You idiot. You're about to ruin this night for both of you.*

"What if he does?" she asked as she kissed his neck.

"You...you don't care?" he panted. She was tickling him with her lips against his skin. It was wet, and warm, and his nerves were firing in every direction.

"Jacob..." she said and then blew air onto his skin. The hair on his skin rose. "You're a horny little boy, aren't you?" she added and kissed his neck again.

"Um..." he said. He struggled to find his words. Sandra nibbled on his ear lobe and Jacob quivered. Then she pulled his hand a little farther under her dress.

"Jacob, I want you to touch me," she said.

"I... I am," he responded.

"You know what I mean," she whispered and plunged his fingers inside her.

"Oh..."

"Feels good doesn't it?" she asked. He nodded.

"Mmhm," he said. Once again, he struggled to find the words to say to her. But this wasn't an instance where words were required. He knew that.

He hadn't been with any women who exhibited such control of the moment. He was used to being the one to make every decision in his interactions with the girls his age. Even with Brea, he had to take the lead, though she was no pushover. Sandra was different. Her experience alone did not suggest her ability to make him do whatever she wanted. And he was willing and ready to do whatever she wanted.

She barely spoke when she suggested they change venues. In fact, he could not remember if she said anything at all. She lowered her legs and pulled on his hand, and he followed along like a dog being ushered by its owner. He followed her into a small room in the back of the house. It was a part of the house he had not been in before. Jacob could not tell what the area looked like as the lights were all turned off.

Sandra did not bother turning the lights on. However, when they entered the room, she lit a small lamp by the table. The light was dim but created a warmly lit atmosphere. Her beauty glowed, even under the spare lighting. Jacob was besides himself. He was further elated when Sandra swiftly removed her dress revealing a well-toned body that left the young man speechless. His imagination could not have conjured her body.

"Do you like my body Jacob?" she asked. He nodded excessively. *Stop acting like an amateur Jacob. Don't be an idiot.*

"Yes," he whispered.

"Take your clothes off," she said. Jacob began taking his clothes off as she lay on the bed, "slowly...so that I can enjoy the beauty of youth," she added. And he obliged.

Jacob carefully removed his clothes, putting them by the side of the door, atop one another. He knew that he had to be strategic about where he put his clothes. Despite the fact that his body was ready to obey each, and every command Sandra gave, his mind was wary of the fact that she did have a husband and he could potentially come into the house at any moment. He had to put his clothes all in one place in case he had to make a hurried exit. And when he was done taking his clothes off, Jacob climbed onto the bed on top of her. Sandra giggled and shook her head.

"Don't be silly Jacob," she said.

"What do you mean?" he asked.

"A man must be willing to please a woman with his lips before he can expect any pleasure," she said as she slowly guided his head downward.

"Oh," he said, "girls don't usually..."

"I'm not a girl," she quickly answered as she opened her legs, "I don't have all night Jacob. And I insist," she added. As he had done before, Jacob obliged.

A little later that night, an exhausted and bemused Jacob trudged out of the Halimut household, wary of the owner coming home. He was lethargic and in a complete haze. He could not fathom what had happened. In fact, he was not sure it happened. Though the pleasure centers in his body were firing on all cylinders, Jacob felt as though he had just done something bad. It was his first time sleeping with someone else's wife. And he enjoyed it. He could not deny that. He enjoyed every part of it. He enjoyed being told what to do by an older woman. He enjoyed being with a woman who demanded what she wanted.

As he walked down the road in a haze, he relived the moments he shared with Sandra. Their time together was unexpected. It was the kind of event a young man dreamed about but seldom got to experience.

The night sky was full of stars so bright that he thought he might be able to touch one just by reaching for it. He could hear the ocean waves crash against the sand as animals of the night made their calling sounds. Occasionally he'd hear sounds of young men and women in a show of overzealous joy. He could not bemoan their excitement. He too was full of joy. He wished the night would not end. He wished he could trap this feeling coursing through his body in a jar and let it out whenever he needed to relive what true joy felt like.

He thought about Brea as he walked down the street. He could not figure out why she was so upset with him earlier. The two of them had not expressed their true feelings to one another. Jacob wondered if Brea cared about him. *How can she care about me? We barely know one another. And... she's nothing like Sandra. God, I don't think any woman is like Sandra. I can still smell her on me.*

Jacob did not want to go to sleep. He would wander the town all night if he didn't think law enforcement would harass him. He was on the highest high of his life. And as he got closer to the bar, he thought more about Brea. He knew she'd already be off work, so it didn't make sense for him to go to the bar.

He called her but she did not answer. He knew then that she must still be upset with him. Or at the minimum she'd be annoyed with him. The way he left her by the bar was not nice. He understood that. Jacob hoped that she had time to think about the way their last conversation went. He hoped she'd have seen that he had no control over whatever Rose told her about the two of them.

Feeling brave and renewed, Jacob decided he had to talk to Brea that night. He could have waited until the morning, but he did not want to leave anything to chance. The alcohol he consumed earlier in the day seemed to have been sapped out of him. He couldn't tell if it was the coffee or the sex that sobered him up. All he was sure of was that his mind was clear. He could see things clearly. So, he headed to the Inn.

The inn was quiet, with very little lighting available. He turned on the flashlight on his phone and used it as a guide to Brea's room. He could see through the edges of the windows that her light was still on. So, he knocked on the door. He heard some footsteps, but the door did not open. So, he knocked again.

"Some people have to sleep around here," she said when she opened the door. She was wearing a long shirt and panties.

"Hi," he said.

"What the hell do you want Jacob?" she said. The door was barely open. He tried to walk in the room, but she pushed the door a little against him.

"I came by to apologize to you," he said. She scoffed. "No seriously, I'm sorry for my behavior earlier. I was drinking a lot and..."

"Jacob, I don't own you. You do whatever the hell you want. Now I want to go to sleep," she said. Jacob took a deep breath.

So, she's going to pretend she really doesn't care about what I'm saying right now. She wants me to beg. Jacob leaned against the wall and slightly put his feet in the doorway. Then he smiled. She frowned. He pretended to pout. Then he reached to grab her shirt and she hit his hand.

"I promise I'm not drunk," he said.

"You smell," she replied. He lifted his arm to smell his armpit.

"Not bad," he said. She tried to close the door again, but he put his hand in the doorway. "Please Brea, I'm sorry. I'm really sorry for the way I acted earlier. I should have listened to you instead of just reacting. Forgive me?" he added.

"Where did you go?" she asked.

"I was just wandering around," he said.

He couldn't tell her the truth. He didn't want to hurt her feelings by telling her he was with another woman. Despite whatever he may have experienced, he could not know for sure whether Brea would have been welcoming of that kind of information. She looked at him as if she was wondering if she believed anything that was coming out of his mouth.

Brea opened the door wider and he entered. She sniffed him as he walked past her, and he laughed. Then she climbed back into her bed where she had left a pile of pop culture magazines. Jacob jumped onto the bed and crawled next to her.

"Boys really do smell awful," she said and laughed as she flipped through pages of the magazine in front of her.

"I think your message is clear," he said. She tapped him on the head.

"Rose..."

"There's nothing there." he said. She smirked.

"Jacob Alexander...your mother must be really proud," she said. He chuckled.

"Brea,"

"Yeah Jacob Alexander?"

"I think I'm in love with you," he said. She scoffed. She patted his head. He reached and tried to kiss her, and she pushed his head to the side.

"Come back to me when you're sure lover boy," she said. Jacob sighed.

CHAPTER 5

The following Monday, Jacob was elated to return to work. There seemed to be a new balance to his time in Greenport and he was more enthusiastic about having to go to the farm. He stopped by Mr. Hagen's table in the front of the Inn, having recently left Brea's room. The older gentleman was wearing blue swim trunks and brown dress shoes with no shirt on. He completed his look with a white hat that had a seashell tucked to the side. Jacob was astounded by the man's eclectic composition of a look. Mr. Hagen lowered his sunglasses and looked at the young man and then smiled.

"You seem much happier young Jacob," Mr. Hagen said, "have a seat, take some coffee with me," he added.

"I'm sorry Mr. Hagen but I have to get to the farm on time today," Jacob replied. Mr. Hagen chuckled.

"There's no use rushing to go work for another man," Mr. Hagen said.

"Oh, Hagen stop bothering the boy, let him go be responsible," Mrs. Conti said as she came out of the front doors.

"Hi Mrs. Conti," Jacob said and kissed her on the cheek.

"Get going boy before you lose your job and I have to kick you out," Mrs. Conti said and chuckled. Jacob winked at Mr. Hagen.

"Love the outfit!" Jacob shouted as he walked away. Mr. Hagen laughed.

Jacob took a taxi to the Halimut farm. He could have walked, but he remembered what Brea said about boys always smelling and so did not want to do anything that would cause him to sweat before he had to start working. He wondered if Sandra would be walking the grounds. She had a habit of going for walks on the grounds and the thought of seeing her made him excited. He knew that what happened between the two of them was a one-time thing. A woman like Sandra was not likely to find him so intriguing a second time around. Jacob was not certain he satisfied her during their time together. Besides, he was growing closer to Brea and Sandra would only prove to be a distraction.

When he arrived at the farm, two men in denim jackets were standing at the front of the entrance to the farm. By the looks of their well-manicured hands, he knew that these men did not work on the farm. He had not seen them before. The dark-haired man put his hand up as Jacob went to open the gate to enter. Then he shook his head.

"Hi, I'm Jacob Alexander, I'm working for Mr. Halimut for the summer," Jacob said. The dark-haired man looked over at the other man. The other man walked toward Jacob.

"I'm Travis Halimut, Brendan told us to have you wait here for him," the man said. Jacob scratched his head. He did not know why Mr. Halimut was having him wait at the gate. He wondered if he was getting a new work assignment. He did not want to have to shovel horse manure.

The dark-haired man got out his phone and dialed. He walked away from the gate so that Jacob could not hear his conversation. Travis stood by the gate, tapping it with his foot as though he was performing a country song in a Nashville dive bar. Jacob took off his bag and put it on the ground. He was getting hot. All his thinking around not sweating was proving to be useless now. The sun was out, and he was going to sweat whether he wanted to or not. Then he saw Luis by the barn he painted. He waved at Luis. Luis waved back sheepishly and then shook his head.

A few minutes later, he saw Mr. Halimut coming in his Jeep. Jacob picked up his bag, under the impression that he was going to be let in so that he could start working. Mr. Halimut had an angry look on his face. His face was red, as though he had spent more than a few minutes in a state of pure rage, or under the morning sun. Jacob looked around. He scratched his head.

"Mr. Halimut, good morning sir," Jacob said.

"You have the nerve to show up here?" Mr. Halimut said as he slowly walked over to the gate. The dark-haired man walked beside him, quietly imploring him to keep his cool.

"Is everything okay?" Jacob asked.

"You think I'm stupid? Is that it? I bring you here, give you a job, some responsibilities and this is how you repay me?" Mr. Halimut asked.

At first Jacob could not quite put the pieces together. He wondered if Rose said something to her father about him. He remembered Brea told him that she and Rose had an altercation. He would not have been surprised to find out that Rose, being upset with whatever happened between her and Brea, said something to her father to suggest that he had done something wrong. He knew that if Mr. Halimut remained calm enough, he would be able to explain that he was not the guilty party. He had done nothing to the man's daughter. He was respectful and pushed Rose away when necessary.

"Mr. Halimut, I promise you I did exactly what you asked me to do. I stayed away from her. I don't even talk to her. Whatever happened between her and Brea had nothing to do with me," Jacob said.

Suddenly Mr. Halimut rushed to the gate and swung at Jacob, who stumbled backwards. Travis grabbed Mr. Halimut and pulled him back. But Mr. Halimut brushed his brother to the side and climbed over the gate. Jacob, on the ground, tried to crawl backwards, but lost his balance and crashed onto the sweltering hot gravel ground. Mr. Halimut climbed on top of the young man.

"You think you can sleep with my wife and show up here like nothing happened?" Mr. Halimut said.

"Your..." Jacob said. He had not finished his sentence when Mr. Halimut's fist crashed against his jaw. Jacob's head flew backwards and hit the gravel ground. And before he could find his focus, another punch crashed against his face. And then another. He could barely raise his hands to protect himself.

Travis and the dark-haired man pulled Mr. Halimut off the young man. Jacob felt blood dribble off his face and down his cheeks. He moved his head from side to side, trying to find his focus. Everything was blurry. He heard multiple voices. It seemed other people had joined to see what was going on. *She told her husband. She told him what happened. Why would she do that? Why would she? Ha-ha, I was right. That woman is dangerous. She played me against her husband. All this time he was worried that someone would try to take advantage of his daughter. He never thought his wife would be taking advantage of others.*

Jacob managed to lift his head a little and slowly lean up. Luis came to his side and sat him up. He could see Rose standing by the gate, aghast and unable to process what she had just seen. Far behind Rose was Sandra, watching on. Of what little Jacob could see, he knew she felt nothing. What her husband had done was no surprise to her. Travis was still holding Mr. Halimut back as some work hands pleaded with their boss to regain his composure.

"You're fired! You hear me?" Mr. Halimut shouted. Jacob heard ringing in his ears. He was still struggling to regain his focus.

Rose ran by her father and came to his side, opposite of Luis. They managed to get Jacob up. Jacob pushed Rose's hands off him. *This family is the literal devil. I can't believe I was so stupid.* Jacob had a smile on his face. He managed to get fired within a few weeks of being at the farm. He knew his mother and his professor would both be disappointed, but he thought it was funny.

"Oh, you think this is a joke?" Mr. Halimut said as he pushed past his brother and headed for Jacob once more.

"Dad! Stop it! You're embarrassing yourself," Rose said, "She's the one who hurt you here. He's just a boy. What is wrong with you?" she added as she pointed at her mother who stood in the background, unmoved by what she was witnessing.

"I'll deal with her when I'm done with him," Mr. Halimut said. Sandra laughed.

"Deal with me? Have you lost your damn mind? You incompetent imbecile. Put your hands on me and see what'll happen," Sandra said.

Wow that is sexy. Maybe I'm a bit sadistic. The power in that woman's tongue is intoxicating. Ha-ha, I'm all beat up and I still find her so sexy.

He smiled again. This time he was directly smiling at her. He didn't care how Mr. Halimut felt about him. He struggled to bend down and grab his bag. Rose stood in front of her father, blocking his access to Jacob.

"You better get out of here before he goes and grabs his gun," Luis whispered to Jacob, "a heartbroken man will do anything," he added. Jacob nodded.

"Thanks," Jacob said.

"I warned you about this," Luis said. Jacob nodded. "Meet up at the bar later?"

"Yeah man. Thanks again," Jacob said.

"Jacob let me get you some gauze at least," Rose said. Jacob shook his head. "Where are you going?"

"Who gives a damn where he goes? You better not ever show your face here again...in fact you better get out of Greenport!" Mr. Halimut said. Travis pulled his brother back.

"Brendan, let the kid go," Travis said.

Jacob had no place in mind when he left the Halimut farm. His face hurt as though he had been hit with a sizable brick. His vision slowly improved as he walked the streets of Greenport, contemplating what to do next. He thought about whether he should stay in Greenport for another month and finish out his summer where he started it. It would mean having to get a job elsewhere so that he could pay for his room at the end. At the very least it would mean having to ask his mother and his sister for money to be able to pay for his stay.

He wasn't sure he wanted to stay in the town. Going back to Oakwood would not be the worst thing he did. He walked to the town center and went to the carousel where he first met Rose and sat on a wooden bench facing the carousel. He watched as young families cajoled their children into getting on the carousel. He couldn't remember if he enjoyed carousels as a child. *I'm not sure why any kid likes a carousel. You always get off a little disoriented.*

He sat there, watching for a while, constantly having to wipe drips of blood off his face. He endured the occasional stare from people who found his bloodied face jarring. There was blood on his shirt, but that seemed inconsequential. Jacob found joy in seeing the reactions of the people who walked by and stared at him.

"Do you need some help, young man?" an elderly woman walking her chocolate lab said as she stopped by the bench.

"No, thank you," Jacob said.

"Are you sure?" she asked. Jacob sighed.

"Yeah, I'm sure," he said. The woman shook her head and walked on.

A few hours later, Jacob grabbed his bag and left the carousel. He walked down the road to the bar where Brea worked. Though it was still early, the place was packed with young people drinking the day away. Unlike the reaction he got from the people around the carousel, people in the bar barely noticed Jacob when he walked through the front door.

Even when he bumped into some young women dancing in the center of the bar, they barely looked at him. He excused himself and went to sit at the bar. He felt great relief when the cool air of the establishment hit his face.

"Jacob what are you...wait what the hell happened to your face?" Brea said when she saw him. She left from behind the bar and walked over to his side.

"I..."

"Oh my God Jacob, who did this to you?" she asked as she kissed his bruised face.

"Mr. Halimut," Jacob said. He was wary of telling her the truth, but he also knew that he didn't care enough to lie about it.

"Why on earth would he do that to you? We need to call the town police, that is ridiculous," she said and kissed him again.

"I slept with his wife," Jacob said. Brea paused. She removed her hand from his face.

"Oh," she said.

"I'm sorry," he said. Brea reached over the counter and grabbed a bottle of rum. Then she grabbed two shot glasses and poured the rum in them. Jacob went to grab a shot glass and she hit his hand. She proceeded to take both shots.

"I'm really sorry," he said and grabbed her hand.

"It's okay Jacob. I already told you, I don't own you. You are your own person and I can't tell you what to do," she said, "can I get you something to drink? Maybe some ice?" she added. He nodded.

A few days later, Jacob was in his room packing his bags when he heard a knock on the door. He looked at the time and thought it was too early for Brea to be at the door. She was supposed to come half an hour later. He was a little annoyed that he had to stop packing to answer the door. *This better not be Mrs. Conti, I already paid her what I owe her.* When he opened the door, it was Rose standing there with a small rectangular box with a bow on top of it in her hand. She wore a blue dress that accentuated her eyes. Jacob looked past her, trying to make sure this wasn't a trap with her father hiding nearby.

"What are you doing here?" he asked. She smiled.

"I can't come say hi to you?" she asked. He continued looking around. "What are you looking for?" she added.

"Your dad," he said. "My face just started feeling better," he added. She chuckled.

"I'm sorry, that's not funny," she said, "can I come in?" she added. He opened the door wider and let her in.

"Seriously, what are you doing here?" he asked.

"Are you going somewhere?"

"I'm leaving, yeah. Being anywhere near your family is detrimental to my health," he said, "plus school starts in a few weeks anyway," he added. She sat on the bed.

"Jacob," she said as he walked into the bathroom to gather his toiletries.

"Yeah?" he shouted from the bathroom.

"I brought you some cake," she said. He chuckled.

"Did your mother bake it?" he asked.

"I don't want to talk about my mother. That's the last thing I want to talk about," she said. He came back into the room.

"I'm sorry. And thank you for the cake," he said.

"My parents are getting divorced," she said. Jacob scratched his chin. He felt bad about having any part to play in the dissolution of a marriage. "Don't worry, it's not because of you. It's been coming for a long time. Those two just aren't...she hasn't been happy for a long time," she added.

"Oh,"

"Jacob, I'm falling in love with you," she said, "I think,"

"Ha-ha," he said.

"It's not funny. I can't control it. All I do is think about you," she said.

"Well, as a friend once told me, come back when you're really sure," he said.

Jacob sat on the bed next to Rose, knowing that he would have to let her down. The fact that she was younger than him did not bother him all that much, but his feelings for Brea had grown. And given what happened between him and Sandra, he didn't think Rose would still be interested in him. She inched closer to him.

"You smell good," she said. He sighed.

"I showered," he said. She laughed.

"Boys always smell bad," she said. He chuckled.

"That's what I keep hearing," he replied. He opened the box.

"It's red velvet. She said you would really like it," she said, "I baked it myself," she added. She moved in to kiss him, but he pulled back.

"I'm sorry Rose. You're a sweet girl, but...I have this thing going on with Brea and I really don't want to mess it up," he said. Rose moved back a little.

"Oh," she said as she played with her hair.

"I'm sorry," he said.

"It's...it's okay. I'm always a few steps behind. I never get what I want," she said.

Jacob thought it quaint that she said that. He had been the one interested in her at the beginning and she rebuffed him. *Maybe she is always a few steps behind. That's not such a bad thing. I wouldn't be any good for her anyway. Her mother was right about her being inexperienced. Plus, I like a woman who goes for what she wants.*

He got up and walked over to the dresser and removed the last few items in there. He had no reservations about having to leave Greenport. The experience was not exactly what he had in mind, but he was okay with how things turned out. He did not like getting beat up by Mr. Halimut, but Jacob enjoyed what led to that end.

"You really baked it?" he asked. She nodded.

"Wanna try?" she asked.

"Yeah, there's a plate and a knife in the cupboard to the left of the sink," he said. Rose walked over to the sink and grabbed the plate and knife. She then opened the box and cut a slice and handed it to him.

"I hope you like it," she said.

"Thank you," he said as he took a bite into the piece of cake, "Listen, you have my contact information. I want you to come see me at school. If you still want to be my friend after all of this," he said. She smiled.

"I don't know if I like you anymore," she said and laughed. He also laughed. "I'd love to come visit you," she added.

"I'd like that,"

There was a knock on the door and Rose lifted her head to get a view through the windows. Jacob got up. He knew who it was. He still had a piece of cake on his fork. When he opened the door, Brea jumped a little and kissed him. Then she noticed Rose sitting on the bed. Brea smiled at her and Rose got up from the bed.

"I didn't know you were here," Brea said.

"She just came by with some cake," Jacob said. Brea walked over to Rose and hugged her.

"No hard feelings," she said. Rose nodded.

"Where are you guys headed?" Rose asked, "are you driving him home?"

"No, we're going to Montauk for a few days and then he's going home," Brea said.

"I just need to finish packing." Jacob said.

Rose stayed for a little longer, talking with Brea while Jacob finished packing his belongings. Jacob thought it was strange that these two young women who were once at odds with one another seemed to have found balance. He looked lovingly at Brea, whom he admired for her ability to not let things bother her.

He thought he'd be more upset about having been fired, but he was not. Jacob was relieved. He hated working on the farm. He'd miss Sandra and how she was as a person. And he'd miss Rose for how she challenged him. Brea had changed his life, even if she was not aware of it.

THE END

71

Thanks for reading!

DID YOU LIKE THIS BOOK?

73

I NEED YOU...

Without reviews, indie books are impossible to market. Leaving a review will only take a minute. It doesn't need to be long, just a sentence or two telling people what you liked about the book. This will give others an idea of why they might like it too. It will also help me in writing more stories about these characters.

Few Rockstar readers leave reviews, and it would mean the world to me if you could be one of those.

Thank You!

Also by Tara C. Goddard

Oakwood
Dorian and Julia: Oakwood Book One
Blue Falls
The Rose Proposal

Standalone
Sandra's Rose

Watch for more at www.tcgoddard.com.

www.ingramcontent.com/pod-product-compliance
Lightning Source LLC
Chambersburg PA
CBHW031500130726
47989CB00003B/1481